TOP 10 GROSSEST ANIMALS

Children's Press®
An imprint of Scholastic Inc.

BY BRENNA MALONEY

A special thank-you to the team at the Cincinnati Zoo & Botanical Garden for their expert consultation.

Copyright © 2025 by Scholastic Inc.

All rights reserved. Published by Children's Press, an imprint of Scholastic Inc., *Publishers since 1920*. SCHOLASTIC, CHILDREN'S PRESS, and associated logos are trademarks and/or registered trademarks of Scholastic Inc.

The publisher does not have any control over and does not assume any responsibility for author or third-party websites or their content.

No part of this publication may be reproduced, stored in a retrieval system, or transmitted in any form or by any means, electronic, mechanical, photocopying, recording, or otherwise, or used to train any artificial intelligence technologies, without written permission of the publisher. For information regarding permission, write to Scholastic Inc., Attention: Permissions Department, 557 Broadway, New York, NY 10012.

Library of Congress Cataloging-in-Publication Data available

ISBN 978-1-5461-3602-6 (library binding)
ISBN 978-1-5461-3603-3 (paperback)

10 9 8 7 6 5 4 3 2 1   25 26 27 28 29

Printed in China   62
First edition, 2025

Book design by Kay Petronio

HOATZIN

HAGFISH

Photos ©: back cover center right: Paul Bersebach/MediaNews Group/Orange County Register/Getty Images; 2 right: Paul Bersebach/MediaNews Group/Orange County Register/Getty Images; 4 left: Carine06/Flickr; 4 top right: Wild Horizons/Universal Images Group/Getty Images; 5 top left: Josh/stock.adobe.com; 5 top center: Cay-Uwe/Getty Images; 5 top right: Paul Souders/Getty Images; 5 bottom center: Doug Perrine/NPL/Minden Pictures; 5 bottom right: Damocean/Getty Images; 8–9: Wirestock/Getty Images; 10–11 main: Wild Horizons/Universal Images Group/Getty Images; 11 bottom right: Discovery Access; 12–13 main: Jean and Fred Hort/Flickr; 14–15 main: Gary Meszaros/Science Source; 15 bottom right: Natural History Collection/Alamy Images; 16–17 main: Kerryn Parkinson/ZUMAPRESS/Newscom; 17 bottom right: Josh/stock.adobe.com; 20–21 main: Josh More/Flickr; 21 bottom right: Mark Newman/Getty Images; 22–23 main: Helmut Corneli/Alamy Images; 23 bottom right: WaterFrame/Alamy Images; 24–25 main: KenCanning/Getty Images; 25 bottom right: George Bloise/Getty Images; 26 main: Elizabeth Beard/Getty Images; 27: Brandon Cole Marine Photography; 28–29: blickwinkel/Alamy Images; 30 top right: Utopia_88/Getty Images; 30 bottom center: Arthur Morris/Getty Images.
All other photos © Shutterstock.

CONTENTS

The World of Gross 4
#10: Hoatzin 6
    Hoatzin Close-Up 8
#9: Desert Horned Lizard 10
#8: Bird-Dropping Spider 12
#7: Hellbender 14
#6: Blobfish 16
#5: Dung Beetle 18
#4: Naked Mole-Rat 20
#3: Sea Cucumber 22
#2: Turkey Vulture 24
#1: Hagfish 26
    Hagfish Close-Up 28
Sizing Them Up 30
Glossary 31
Index/About the Author 32

THE WORLD OF GROSS

DESERT HORNED LIZARD

BIRD-DROPPING SPIDER

HOATZIN

HELLBENDER

There are so many gross animals in our wild world! Some smell bad. Some are slimy. Some like to eat icky things. Some are snotty, squishy, or even rotten!

But . . . are you ready to discover which one is the absolute grossest? Read on and count down from ten to one to learn which animal takes the top spot!

TURKEY VULTURE

BLOBFISH

DUNG BEETLE

NAKED MOLE-RAT

HAGFISH

SEA CUCUMBER

#10
HOATZIN
(ho-AT-zin)

SMELLY!

FACT FILE

ANIMAL GROUP: Bird

HABITATS: Fresh water, forests, swamps

AVERAGE SIZE: A windshield wiper

DIET: Herbivore

What is that smell? It is the hoatzin. This gross bird smells like poop! It is one of the few birds that only eats leaves. It snips off tree leaves with its strong beak. Then the food drops down into the bird's crop.

The crop is a food pouch in its chest. **Bacteria** breaks down the food. This gives the bird gas. The gas makes it burp! So, *that* is what you are smelling!

FACT The name hoatzin can also be pronounced "waht-SEEN."

HOATZIN CLOSE-UP

WINGS
Wings are not used much for flying. This bird mostly hops from tree branch to tree branch.

TAIL
A long, wide tail helps with balance.

FACT: Hoatzins have many nicknames: skunk bird, stinkbird, and stinky turkey!

HEAD
Stiff, orange feathers stand straight up.

EYES
Red, round eyes can see well.

FACE
Blue skin covers its face.

CROP
A food pouch helps **digest** food.

#9 DESERT HORNED LIZARD

BLOODY!

FACT FILE
- **ANIMAL GROUP:** Reptile
- **HABITAT:** Deserts
- **AVERAGE SIZE:** A computer mouse
- **DIET:** Carnivore

When the desert horned lizard gets scared, watch out! It squirts blood from its eyes. Gross! How does it happen? The lizard squeezes the muscles around its eyes.

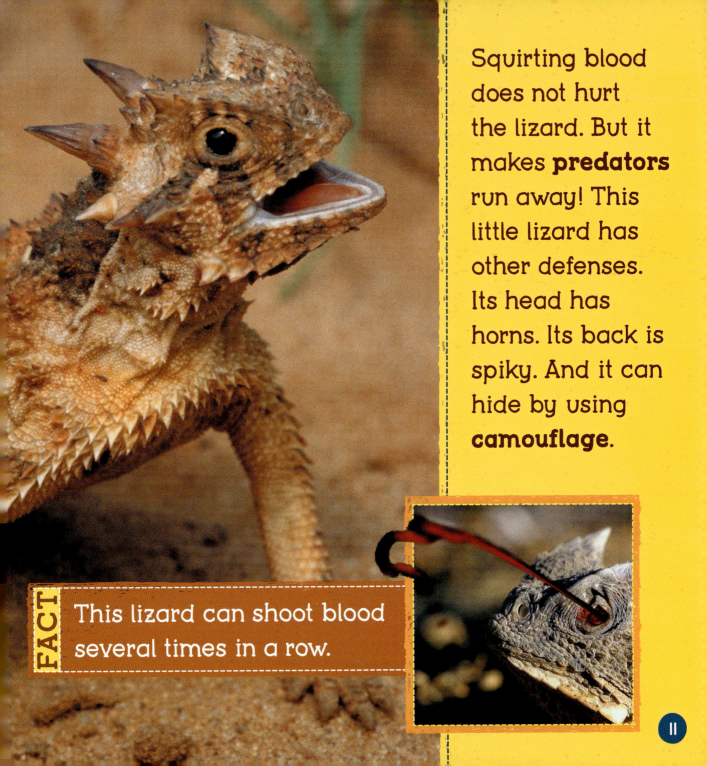

Squirting blood does not hurt the lizard. But it makes **predators** run away! This little lizard has other defenses. Its head has horns. Its back is spiky. And it can hide by using **camouflage**.

FACT This lizard can shoot blood several times in a row.

#8 BIRD-DROPPING SPIDER

GOOEY!

FACT FILE

ANIMAL GROUP: Invertebrate

HABITATS: Gardens and woodlands

AVERAGE SIZE: A quarter

DIET: Carnivore

The bird-dropping spider does not want to be eaten. How does it hide? It looks like bird poop! This gross-looking spider is black, brown, and white. It sits on leaves. Its lumpy body looks wet.

It tucks its legs close to its body to hide them. It sits still. This camouflage fools predators. From the air, hungry birds do not see a spider. They see something they *do not* want to eat!

FACT This spider also makes a white silk to sit on.

#7 HELLBENDER
SNOTTY!

FACT FILE

ANIMAL GROUP: Amphibian

HABITAT: Fresh water

AVERAGE SIZE: A desk lamp

DIET: Carnivore

A hellbender is also called a snot otter. Good luck trying to grab this amphibian! Its skin is coated in a thick **mucus**. It is too slippery to hold on to. This "snot" helps it slip away from predators.

A hellbender also tastes bitter. Predators spit it out! It might seem gross to be covered in snot. But snot protects its skin. It blocks harmful bacteria that could make a hellbender sick.

FACT Hellbenders are also called "mud cats"!

#6 BLOBFISH
MUSHY!

FACT FILE

- **ANIMAL GROUP:** Fish
- **HABITAT:** Oceans
- **AVERAGE SIZE:** A football
- **DIET:** Omnivore

Why does a blobfish look like it is frowning? It has droopy skin. But only when it is out of water. Blobfish live deep in the ocean. The water pressure is heavy.

This blobfish is out of water.

The pressure holds the shape of the blobfish's body. When it comes up to the surface, the water pressure is gone. The blobfish's skin becomes loose. Its body starts to look like a "blob"!

FACT: The blobfish has been called the "world's ugliest animal."

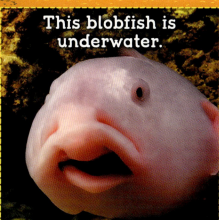

This blobfish is underwater.

#5 DUNG BEETLE

STINKY!

FACT FILE

ANIMAL GROUP: Invertebrate

HABITATS: Deserts, grasslands, forests, savannas

AVERAGE SIZE: A large grape

DIET: Dung

A dung beetle is never far from dung. That means animal poop. This beetle moves dung. It lives in it. It eats it. Gross! This beetle shapes pieces of dung into balls. It rolls the ball away from the dung pile.

Then, it buries the dung by digging under the pile. Female dung beetles lay their eggs there. When the eggs hatch, the young start munching on the dung. *Nom nom nom!*

FACT Dung beetles are strong. They can move balls of dung that are bigger and heavier than they are.

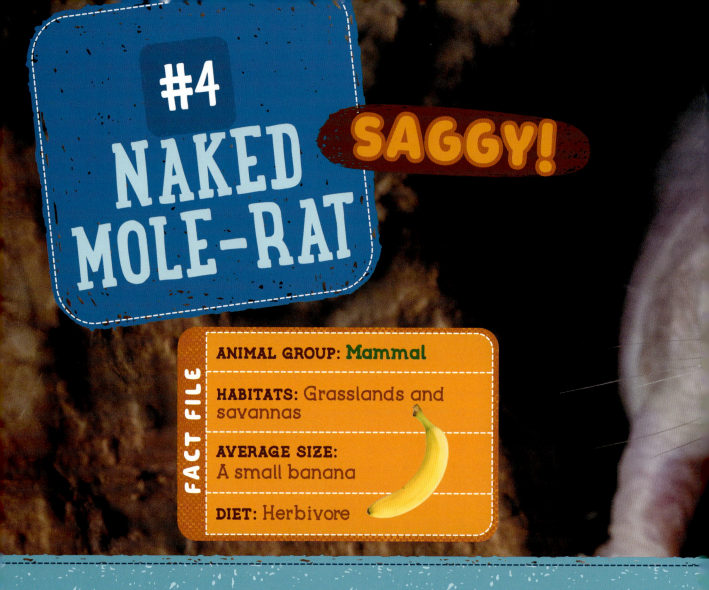

#4 NAKED MOLE-RAT

SAGGY!

FACT FILE

ANIMAL GROUP: Mammal

HABITATS: Grasslands and savannas

AVERAGE SIZE: A small banana

DIET: Herbivore

Meet the naked mole-rat! This hairless **rodent** lives underground in large groups called colonies. A naked mole-rat has tiny eyes and big front teeth. It is covered in pinkish-gray, baggy skin.

This mammal looks like an uncooked sausage. And it eats its own poop! A naked mole-rat is as unusual as it is gross. It can live without air for almost 20 minutes.

FACT A naked mole-rat colony **burrow** can be as long as 2.5 miles (4 km).

#3 SQUISHY! SEA CUCUMBER

FACT FILE

- **ANIMAL GROUP:** Invertebrate
- **HABITAT:** Oceans
- **AVERAGE SIZE:** A pickle
- **DIET:** Scavenger

Most animals keep their insides *inside*. Not sea cucumbers! This squishy animal is found on the ocean floor. It shovels food into its mouth with tiny, tube-like feet.

To avoid being eaten, a sea cucumber does something gross. It can shoot some of its **organs** out of its back end. A predator will stop to eat the organs. This allows the sea cucumber to escape! It can regrow the parts it left behind.

FACT: Sea cucumbers do not have a brain, heart, or lungs.

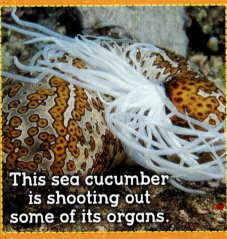

This sea cucumber is shooting out some of its organs.

#2 TURKEY VULTURE

ROTTEN!

FACT FILE

ANIMAL GROUP: Bird

HABITAT: Forests

AVERAGE SIZE: A large backpack

DIET: Scavenger

Never accept a lunch invitation from a turkey vulture. It only eats things that are rotten. It can smell rotten animals from a mile (1.6 km) away. A turkey vulture will poke its head into a smelly meal.

Then it uses its sharp beak to eat. Its head is bald, so nothing can stick to its feathers. This bird might be gross, but it does an important job! Eating rotten animals helps stop diseases from spreading.

FACT A scared turkey vulture might vomit on a predator!

#1 HAGFISH

SLIMY!

FACT FILE

- **ANIMAL GROUP:** Fish
- **HABITAT:** Oceans
- **AVERAGE SIZE:** A skateboard
- **DIET:** Scavenger

The grossest animal lives underwater! A hagfish only eats dead things. It dives into its food face-first. Then it eats the food from the inside out. If another animal tries to steal its meal, a hagfish fights back.

The hagfish fires off a thick cloud of slime. The slime jets out from the sides of its body. The slime chokes and confuses the other animal. A hagfish is gross, but it is also useful. It helps clean up dead animals from the seafloor.

FACT Hagfish are also called "slime eels" or "snot snakes." But they are not eels or snakes!

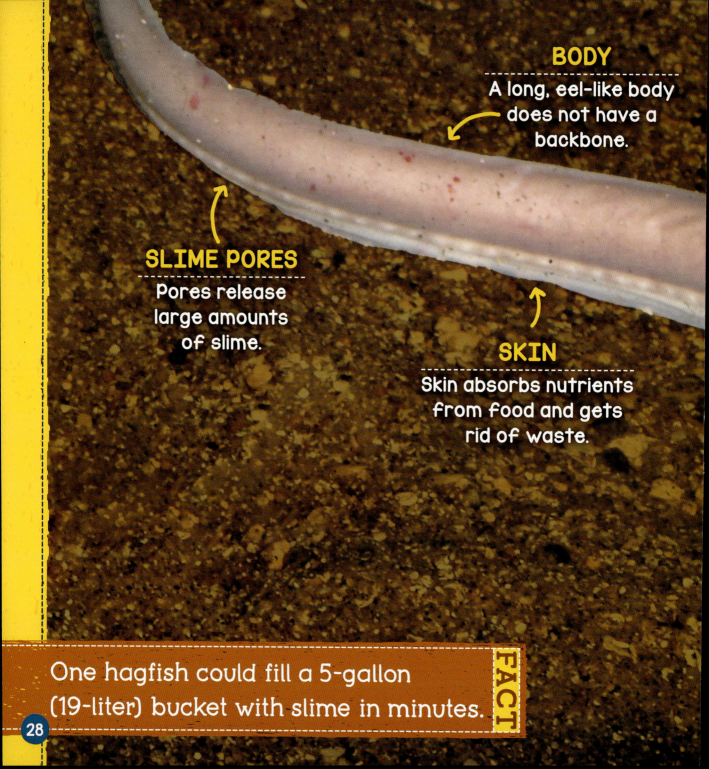

BODY
A long, eel-like body does not have a backbone.

SLIME PORES
Pores release large amounts of slime.

SKIN
Skin absorbs nutrients from food and gets rid of waste.

FACT: One hagfish could fill a 5-gallon (19-liter) bucket with slime in minutes.

HAGFISH CLOSE-UP

ORGANS
Hagfish have four hearts and two brains.

EYESPOTS
Hagfish have poor vision but can sense light.

GILLS
Water exits from its gills.

WHISKERS
Three pairs of whiskers taste and touch.

MOUTH
Four sets of teeth on the tongue help tear food.

SIZING THEM UP

There are so many gross animals in our wild world! They are snotty. They stink. They shoot out clouds of slime. Do you agree the hagfish is the grossest? Or would you pick a different animal? You can probably find even more gross animals and make your own list!

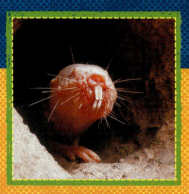

GLOSSARY

amphibian (am-FIB-ee-uhn) a cold-blooded animal with a backbone that lives in water and breathes with gills when young

bacteria (bak-TEER-ee-uh) microscopic, single-cell living things that are everywhere and can either be useful or harmful

burrow (BUR-oh) a tunnel or hole in the ground made or used as a home for an animal

camouflage (KAM-uh-flahzh) a disguise or natural coloring that allows animals to hide

carnivore (KAHR-nuh-vor) an animal that eats meat

digest (dye-JEST) to break down food so that it can be used by the body

herbivore (HUR-buh-vor) an animal that only eats plants

invertebrate (in-VUR-tuh-brit) an animal without a backbone

mammal (MAM-uhl) a warm-blooded animal that has hair or fur and usually gives birth to live babies

mucus (MYOO-kuhs) a thick, slimy liquid that coats and protects

omnivore (AHM-nuh-vor) an animal that eats both plants and meat

organ (OR-guhn) a part of the body, such as the heart or kidneys, that has a certain purpose

predator (PRED-uh-tur) an animal that lives by hunting other animals for food

reptile (REP-tile) a cold-blooded animal that crawls across the ground or creeps on short legs; most have backbones and reproduce by laying eggs

rodent (ROH-duhnt) a mammal with large front teeth that are constantly growing and used for gnawing things

scavenger (SKAV-uhn-jur) an animal that usually feeds on dead or decaying matter

INDEX

Page numbers in **bold** indicate images.

A
amphibians. *See* hellbender

B
bird-dropping spider, **4**, 12–13, **12-13**, **30**
birds. *See* hoatzin; turkey vulture
blobfish, **5**, 16–17, **16-17**

C
camouflage, 11, 13
carnivores. *See* bird-dropping spider; desert horned lizard; hellbender

D
desert animals. *See* desert horned lizard; dung beetle
desert horned lizard, **4**, 10–11, **10-11**, **30**
dung beetle, **5**, 18–19, **18-19**, **30**

F
fish. *See* blobfish; hagfish
forest animals. *See* dung beetle; hoatzin; turkey vulture

freshwater animals. *See* hellbender; hoatzin

G
garden animals. *See* bird-dropping spider
grassland animals. *See* dung beetle; naked mole-rat

H
hagfish, **5**, 26–29, **26-29**
  slime, 27, 28
hellbender, **4**, 14–15, **14-15**
herbivores. *See* hoatzin; naked mole-rat
hoatzin, **4**, 6–9, **6-9**
  crop, 6–7, 9

I
invertebrates. *See* bird-dropping spider; dung beetle; sea cucumber

M
mammals. *See* naked mole-rat

N
naked mole-rat, **5**, 20–21, **20-21**, **30**

O
ocean animals. *See* blobfish; hagfish; sea cucumber
omnivores. *See* blobfish

R
reptiles. *See* desert horned lizard

S
savanna animals. *See* dung beetle; naked mole-rat
scavengers. *See* hagfish; sea cucumber; turkey vulture
sea cucumber, **5**, 22–23, **22-23**
swamp animals. *See* hoatzin

T
turkey vulture, 5, 24–25, **24-25**, **30**

W
woodland animals. *See* bird-dropping spider

ABOUT THE AUTHOR

Brenna Maloney is the author of many books. She lives in Washington, DC, with her husband and two sons. She's fond of dung beetles but thinks naked mole-rats really are pretty gross.